Phartman

By

Glyn Davies

Copyright © 2023 by Glyn Davies

All rights reserved, no part of this book may be used or reproduced in any form whatsoever without written permission except in the case of brief quotations in critical articles or reviews

This book is a work of fiction. No names characters, businesses, organisations, places, events, and incidents either are the product of the authors imagination or are used fictitiously. any resemblance to actual persons, living or dead, events, or locales is entirely coincidental

Printed in the UK

For more information, contact:

glyngregdavies@gmail.com

www.glyndaviesbooks.com

Book design by Glyn Davies

Cover design by Robin Davies

ISBN- paperback **979-8858897385**

ISBN- Kindle B0CH2FBH4W

ISBN- Audible

First edition 2023

The phone rang in Tollpiddle Police Station, and Sgt Randall, who was on duty, picked it up to hear a frantic voice on the other end.

"There's a spaceship in my field, with a green man standing next to it".

Sgt Randall shook his head, "Is that you Geoff? It's not April fools' day till next week".
He put the phone down, which immediately rang again.

"There's a spaceman standing in my field looking at my cabbages," said Geoff, sounding even more excited.

"Geoff, I'm busy".

"Charlie, there's a spaceman, he's walking towards me. Help! Help!"

"Geoff, are you serious?"

"Course I'm serious, come quick, I'm in the bottom field."

Charlie grabbed the keys to the police pick up and drove quickly up to Spinney Hill Farm. Driving over the brow of the hill, he stopped dead in the middle of the cattle grid.

There in the middle of the field was a large silver tube-shaped spacecraft, hovering a few feet above the ground. Halfway between Charlie and the spacecraft was a tall pale green human-like figure dressed in a green suit, quite slim apart from a rather large round bottom, and wearing what looked like a belt with pouches fitted around it. He stood waving towards Charlie whilst inspecting Geoff's cabbages. Geoff came charging over in his tractor. He stopped next to the cattle grid and leapt out to come running over to Charlie.

"Charlie, he's over there! What are you going to do? Go and arrest him, he's squashed my cabbages!"

Charlie sat in his truck wondering what he was going to do, he really wanted to drive off as quickly as possible whilst shouting "THERE'S A SPACMAN IN GEOFF'S FIELD".

But he knew that as a Police Officer, he had to come up with a plan to deal with this strange intruder. Just for a second, he shut his eyes, then opened them again.

To his disappointment the spaceman was still there – he wasn't dreaming it.

They both looked to see the spaceman walking towards them, holding up a hand and waving as he drew closer. Geoff ran round and jumped into the passenger seat of Charlie's truck then locked the door.

Approaching Charlie's window, the spaceman smiled, then said "Gonklespank". Charlie looked at Geoff.

"Not a clue," said Charlie.

The spaceman tapped a panel on his left wrist. "Sorry my translator is set to Grundeslaten on the planet Bumfink. I come in pees". He tapped his wrist panel again. "Sorry, I come in peace, my spacecraft has run out of power, the farting clapper valve is broken, so we have run out of fuel".

"There's a garage about three miles down the road," said Charlie, pointing in the direction of Scratchit village.

"Let me introduce myself," said the spaceman,

"My name is, Phartman Blowbum Pooply Plop, but you can call me Phartman for short, although my friends just call me Pharty".

"FARTMAN," said Charlie.

"Yes Inspector, that's P H A R T M A N. I'm from the planet Gaseous."

"OK..." said Charlie, feeling a little less scared, "what are you doing here in Geoff's cabbage field?"

"Ah, my spacecraft is powered by plants, the Gronkelbonkslapenfurt converts them into power, but the farting clapper valve is broken, so we have run out of fuel, we don't have enough to leave your planet."

"So, what are you doing in my field?" said Geoff.

"We can use your cabbages as fuel, Nik Nik can adjust the Gronkelbonkslapenfurt to run on them," said Phartman.

"You mean there are more of you!" exclaimed Charlie.

"Only Nik Nik," said Phartman, pointing to a small round green hairy ball standing in the field.

It had purple feet and hands, bright yellow eyes and one large tooth in its mouth and wearing a chef's hat.

"What on earth is that?" said Charlie.

"He's not from Earth," said Phartman, "He's a Nikenscartennicbum, but I call him Nik Nik for short. He's the spacecraft's engineer."

"What's he doing? I'm going to chase him off my cabbages," said Geoff, pointing to the little green alien who was now busy poking his cabbages.

"DON'T DO THAT!" yelled Phartman suddenly, making the two men jump in surprise. Holding up a hand to Geoff, he continued, "He's from the planet Guzunder. They are very clever, but very grumpy, best to be avoided. He's been with me a few years now. He's quite good, he only bites me every few weeks now, instead of at every opportunity."

"Well how many of my cabbages do you want?" said Geoff.

"We'll take them all," said Phartman.

"Well OK," said Geoff, "They're not good

enough to sell so you've saved me a job of getting rid of them."

Phartman was delighted, he tapped on his wrist panel and waved to Nik Nik, who jumped up and down making a strange "Bink Bink" sound. Next there seemed to be a small square craft that came out from the back of the spacecraft.

"That's the Slurpen Gulpen collector," said Phartman. "It's going to collect all the fuel; I must give you something in exchange." He reached into one of the pouches on his belt and pulled out a curly pipe that looked like it had been made from rock. "Here, let me give you this, it's a Clackenhurst Horn. The Werrarwies use them to scare off wild elephants."

Charlie looked at it. "We don't get a lot of wild elephants round here".

"Oh, fascinating, what do you use then to keep them away?" asked Phartman.

Charlie looked wearily at Geoff. "Why did you ring today? It's my day off tomorrow."

Within minutes the field was clear.

"What now then?" asked Charlie.

8

"Well Nik Nik will have to adjust the Gronkelbonkslapenfurt drive to run on this new fuel." Said Phartman.

"Well how long will that take?" said Charlie.

"About two to three days."

"Two to three days!" exclaimed Charlie. "Well, you can't stop here. We will be overrun with press reporters and television. You'll have to stop at the police station, you can hide in the back yard."

Charlie gave him the directions, which Phartman typed into his wrist panel. He then turned to wave some signals to Nik Nik.

"Why is he wearing a chef's hat? I thought you said he was the engineer," said Charlie.

"I told you he was clever, he's Co Pilot, Engineer, Navigator, Scientist, Doctor and Chef."

"Well, what do *you* do?" asked Charlie. Phartman stood up straight.

"I've got the most important job. As Captain, I sit in the captain's seat, then when we are ready for take-off, I push a big green button".

"Is that it?" said Geoff.

Phartman raised a pointed finger. "Ah no, when we land, I have to push a big green button, but then I have to turn a round switch as well, so that's why I'm Captain".

Charlie turned to Geoff. "Are you anything to do with this? I told you April Fool's Day isn't till next week".

"No, no I drove down the road this morning and there he was," insisted Geoff. Charlie turned back to talk to Phartman, but he had gone.

"Where's the spaceship?" shouted Charlie, he turned to Geoff. "OK what have you done with it".

"Honestly, it's nothing to do with me, look all my cabbages have gone."

They both sat looking at the space in the field where the spaceship had been standing. Charlie was hoping this was all a dream and he would wake up with everything being normal. He was suddenly shaken out of his daydream as his police radio burst into life.

"SARGE, SARGE, where are you?" came a frantic voice.

"I'm up at Spinney Farm with Geoff," replied Charlie.

"You had better get back to the police station quick!" said the frantic voice on the radio.

"Dave, what's happened?" asked Charlie.

"I don't want to say over the radio, but everybody has run off, I'm the only one here and I've locked myself in the toilet," came the reply.

"PHARTMAN," said Charlie in a loud voice. "Where is he?"

"He's in the back yard with his angry little mate.

The little green monster bit Pete and Stuart.

Pete tried to taser him, but he just ate the taser."

"Stay where you are, I'm on my way".

Charlie left Geoff in his field and sped back to the police station. He didn't use his siren as he did not want to draw attention to himself.

"Dave, Dave you in there?" shouted Charlie as he approached the men's toilets.

"Yes. Have they gone?" came the reply.

"Well, I can't find them, where were they?" asked Charlie.

"They were in the back yard," Dave said, sheepishly coming out of the toilet.

"Well, they're not there now. They must have gone," said Charlie.
Dave looked out the window into the back yard.

"I hope they've gone for good; I definitely don't want to bump into the little green one again," he said.

"Well come on then, let's go and have a look," said Charlie.
Dave drew out his truncheon to protect himself, slowly opened the back door of the station, then carefully peered round the side.

"Phew, they're gone," he said.

"OK, let's have a good look," said Charlie. They both stepped out into the back yard to look around.

"Where were they?" asked Charlie.

"They were over there by the fence," Dave replied.

Dave stood by the door as Charlie walked over towards the back fence. Then Charlie suddenly stopped as though he had walked into a glass wall. He stepped back then put his hand out in front of him, it stopped on something invisible. He rubbed his hand across it then knocked on it with his knuckles. Suddenly Phartman appeared from a door that seemed to open from nowhere.

Phartman was standing in the doorway to his spacecraft.

"Ah, there you are Inspector!" exclaimed Phartman.

"AAAH, he's still here!" shouted Dave, who took six steps backwards.

"Where's your little green mate?"

"It's OK, I've shut him in the kitchen, he's eating some gangleberries. He gets grumpy when he's hungry," said Phartman.

"Where's your spaceship?" asked Charlie, "I thought you had gone". Phartman tapped his wrist panel, suddenly the spaceship appeared in the back yard.

"WHOA, where did that come from?" said Dave.

"It's from the planet Gaseous, which is nicilyciggy, niclilyciggy, nicy. A long way from Earth," said Phartman.

"Well, what are you doing here?" asked Dave.

"We were on our way to visit the weararwies to collect more fuel, but we started running out, so we had to stop here."

"The weararwies?" repeated Charlie, thoroughly confused.

"They are an unknown tribe who live deep in the Amazon jungle."

"Well, I've never heard of them," said Charlie.

"Yes, that's because they're unknown. I've only ever met two of them. They are only four feet tall but live in dense five-foot-high jungle, so you only hear them, shouting out to

each other in the jungle, 'Where are we'. We used to get the bumbumba fruit for fuel from the Incas in Peru. They would give us fruit and we would build some stone temples for them. It's a shame they all left on a spaceship to live on Nagglslop. That's a small planet in the Slaglog system – nice planet but they can't grow the bumbumba fruit there. Well, Inspector, can we stay here till Nik Nik repairs the Gronkelbonkslapenfurt hyper drive?"
Charlie pointed to his left sleeve.

"Look, three stripes, I'm a sergeant." Phartman looked at Charlie,

"Oh, you're confused now, I'm not three stripes, I'm Phartman".

"What, did you just say… Phartman?" exclaimed Dave.

"Yes, P.H.A.R.T.M.A.N. Although my friends just call me Pharty," said Phartman proudly.

"OK," said Charlie, "It looks like we are stuck with you. Just keep out of the way, we don't want to panic people".

"You won't know we are here, Captain," said Phartman, and just as he did so, a loud rasping sound could be heard coming from the back of the spaceship.

"What was that?" shouted Dave in a panic.

"That's Nik Nik venting the last of the bumbumba fruit from the willyconk tank". Dave started coughing.

"What's that smell? It's horrible!" he said, fishing a tissue from his pocket to hold to his nose.

"It's the bumbumba fruit from the weararwies. It's excellent fuel but a bit smelly to earth people. Nik Nik loves them. We would have had enough fuel if Nik Nik hadn't eaten so many."

"No wonder he's grumpy, if he eats those," said Dave.

"OK, we are going to lock the gates at the front to keep people out," said Charlie.

"And keep you in," added Dave.

"You can trust me, Major," said

Phartman.

"It's Sergeant," Charlie corrected.

"Yes, I suppose it is, Captain, but we can keep warm inside the spacecraft".
Dave turned to Charlie, bewildered.

"Don't ask," was all Charlie could say.

Dave walked backwards into the police station, not wanting to run into the little green monster again. Charlie followed him in and told all the officers and staff not to mention Phartman to anybody.

"We don't want the world's press and television outside tomorrow."
Phartman's spaceship continued to rumble gurgle and blow out some rather unpleasant smells. No one would volunteer to stand guard in the back yard, so an observation post was set up in an upstairs office.

***

June stood in the park blowing her dog whistle, it was twenty minutes since her dog Poppy had run off into the trees chasing a rabbit. She kept looking into the distance looking to see if Poppy had run further down the field. She kept shouting Poppy's name and blowing her whistle but there was no sign of her dog. Whilst watching other dog walkers in the distance, something caught her attention off to the right in the trees. She turned to see a tall figure walking towards her. As he exited the trees, June got a good look at this strange figure.

"You're Phartman!" exclaimed June. Phartman smiled.

"I am that very person; how did you know?"

"Carla in the library told me this morning. She said you walked into the pub last night. Everybody in the village knows about you now." Phartman was carrying a bunch of wild roses in his hand.

"They're lovely, aren't they?" said June.

Phartman looked at them.

"Yes, they are, they're delicious".
Then promptly bit the heads off and ate them.

June's eyes widened as he finished them off by eating the storks.

"These green sticks are really crunchy; you must try some", said Phartman.

"No thanks, I've not long had breakfast", said June. She looked down the park again and blew her whistle, "POPPY, POPPY" she shouted.

"You seem a little worried," said Phartman.

"It's my dog, Poppy. She ran off after a rabbit and I can't get her back," said June anxiously.

"Well, your pipe seems a little out of tune," said Phartman.

June was surprised. "You can hear it?".

"Yes".

"It's my dog whistle. She normally comes back when I blow it, but it doesn't seem to be working".

"Well, your whistle is a bit quiet as well as out of tune," Phartman informed her.

"I don't know what to do," said June.

"Here let me help you", said Phartman.

"We have a way of attracting the Oomigooliey birds on Snagthrap, which is a small planet in the edge of the Bozwalegup system. We use their tail feathers for tickling the feet of baby Nikenrootennikbums. It stops them from biting you. I tried it on Nik Nik, but he just ate it, together with my glove."

Phartman reached into one of his pouches and took out a selection of small berries the size of marbles. He carefully selected four types.

"Oh yes, one of these as well, this should work. How old is your dog?" he enquired.

"About three years old." said June, looking puzzled.

"Hmm, in that case then I'll try one of these". Phartman picked out a small green and yellow berry. "That should work".

June watched as Phartman proceeded to eat all the berries.

"Right, I think I may need the Grapplegrunten pole for this".

He reached around to back of his belt and took out a short tube about the width of a broom handle, he gave it a shake and it suddenly extended in length to about five feet long. Phartman took a step forward with his right foot, then jabbed the Grapplegrunten pole into the ground.

"You may want to take a step back madam," he said.
June was happy to oblige. Phartman put his left hand on his hip, then took a firm grip on the Grapplegrunten pole with his right hand. He leaned slightly forward then, raising one eyebrow, he tilted his head slightly to the left. He held up a hand to June indicating her not to move then, with a frown on his face, he stared up at the sky. June stood watching. wondering what on earth was going to happen next, when a high pitched "Weeeeooooiiiiiiiioooooeeeeepeee" sound came from Phartman's bottom.

June stood riveted to the spot, as the sound like air being released from a balloon being squeezed from the neck continued.

It went on for 10-20 seconds before finishing with a peep and a rasp. Phartman stepped back and stood up straight. He smiled and, nodding his head at June.

"Well, that was excellent, I'm sure that will do the trick."

June stood motionless not sure what she had just witnessed. Her wonderment was suddenly shaken by the sound of barking in the distance, "wuf bark woof woof bark yap woof yap wuf wuf". The sound was getting louder. As she looked, she could see dogs approaching at speed from every direction. "Woof bark yap bark woof woof". Phartman casually put away his Grapplegrunten pole, as the dogs got ever closer. June spotted her dog approaching from the trees.

"POPPY, POPPY!" shouted June as her dog excitedly ran back to her.

Within minutes they were surrounded by twenty-five dogs, three squirrels, two small deer and a goat.

"Wow you've got a lot of pets," said Phartman.

"They're not all mine. Where have the come from?" asked June in astonishment.
She looked down the field to see more dogs dragging their owners hanging onto their leads.

"What are we going to do about this lot?" shouted June over the noise of all the animals. She bent down and put her own dog back on her lead. Phartman surveyed the surrounding chaos, to see more dogs and even a badger approaching, together with some angry dog walkers chasing after their own dogs.
Phartman stood looking for a short time, then turned to June.

"I know exactly what to do," he said, "RUN!"
With that he turned and ran towards the hedge at the edge of the field. To June's amazement, he leapt over the eight-foot hedge and disappeared.

June stood looking in horror as Phartman disappeared over the hedge.

By now she could see several dog owners walking towards her to retrieve their dogs. She quickly picked up Poppy then, reaching into her pocket, she grasped a handful of dog treats and threw them out into the park. Taking advantage of the ensuing chaos, as dogs chased after the free offerings, she made a run for the park gate a short distance away. She quickly shut the gate behind her, then turned and walked off in the direction of the police station.

***

Phartman climbed over the back fence into the police station yard, and quickly stepped into the spacecraft to avoid being seen by a Police Constable escorting some council workmen around the back yard.

The council workmen were there inspecting the drains after complaints about the smell coming from the yard. Graham the Police Constable was carefully ushering them around the yard, making sure he kept himself between them and the invisible spaceship.

"Well, we can't find anything wrong

here," said one of the workmen. "We will have to look further along the estate".

"Great," said Graham, glancing backwards to make sure Phartman was not visible to the workmen.

Just as they walked out the gate, Nik Nik came out of the spaceship with what looked like a long probe. Graham immediately ran into the police station and locked the door. He had met Nik Nik earlier by accident; Nik Nik had run towards him waving what looked like a long vegetable. Graham had panicked and pulled out his truncheon to protect himself, but Nik Nik just bit the end off. Graham dropped what was left of it and ran to the nearest door, locking it behind him.

Charlie came on duty to hear stories of Phartman in the park and the pub.

Now Nik Nik was terrorising people in the back yard.

He was not in the best of moods due to his day off being cancelled because of Phartman.

After the daily briefing to the police officers on duty, he went into the back yard to talk to Phartman. Nik Nik was busy pushing a long rod into the back of the spaceship and didn't notice Charlie. He knocked on the side of the spaceship, the door opened and Phartman stood there smiling.

"Good morning Inspector, come in".

Charlie stepped cautiously into the doorway, looking around to see a vast space inside. He stopped then stepped outside again to look at the outside of the spaceship before stepping back inside.

"That corridor stretches out into the middle of the park, but the outside doesn't even reach the police station fence," said Charlie in amazement.

"Ah that's the visual space thingy wotsit, thing," said Phartman.

"What?" said Charlie.

"I don't know either. Nik Nik presses some buttons and twiddles some switches and things happen," said Phartman.

"How on earth did you manage to get here?" asked Charlie.

"Well Nik Nik presses some buttons and twiddles some switches," Phartman replied.

"But you're the captain," said Charlie.

"Yes of course, I have to press the big red button," said Phartman proudly.

Charlie was about to ask another question when Nik Nik appeared at the door. He looked angrily at Charlie and took a step towards him. Charlie turned to face him.

"You take one more step and I'll kick you into orbit, you nasty little hairy ball of bum fluff," said Charlie pointing a finger at Nik Nik.

Nik Nik stood looking at Charlie for a moment, then turned and walked off down the corridor.

"Well Commander, I've never seen that before, I was expecting him to come and bite your kneecaps. He does usually. What's your secret?"

"Twenty-two years of dealing with yobs and idiots," said Charlie.

"Well, the council members on Guzunder will be very impressed. Do you want a job?

They need someone like you to control the Nikenscartennicbum's. Did I mention to you they can be very grumpy?" said Phartman.

"Yes, you have, and I think Pete and Stuart will vouch for him being a little grumpy, especially as he bit the knees out of their trousers. That's going to make interesting reading when they fill in the request for new ones."

"Well, if you change your mind, let me know," said Phartman, "Come and sit down, let me show you our control station".

Charlie followed Phartman into the control room at the front of the spacecraft, where there were two comfy padded seats looking out to the front, which seemed to be floating, as they were not fixed to the floor. The left-hand seat was surrounded by a curved worktop, covered in dials, gauges, screens, switches, knobs, levers. buttons, beacons, and a vast array of different coloured lights.

"That's Nik Nik's seat. This is mine here," said Phartman, pointing to the right-hand seat. Charlie looked to see it only had two large buttons, one red and one green with one small switch which could turn left or right.

"Shouldn't you be sitting in the left-hand seat?" said Charlie.

"Oh no, I'm the captain. Nik Nik just does some stuff over there. But I have the most important job of pushing the big red button," said Phartman proudly.
Charlie looked back across to the left-hand controls again.

"Yes, I can see that," he said, not wanting to confuse matters even more. "I came to see you, because you caused a bit of trouble in the park this morning. We had a few complaints about your dog calling.

"Why would June complain? I got her dog to come back to her." said Phartman.

"No, not June, we've had a few from the park staff, the badger got into a fight with a bulldog and wrecked a flower bed, the deer ate all the leaves on some new sapling trees just planted and the goat ate all the tulips that had just come into flower.

The Park staff are a miserable bunch at the best of times without you upsetting them," said Charlie.

"I must go and apologise," said Phartman.

"No need for that. From what I've heard, it sounded hilarious, I wish I had seen it." said Charlie.

"You have a strange way of dealing with things," observed Phartman.

"You need a strange way of looking at life in my job," said Charlie. "What's this I hear about you being in the pub last night? So much for keeping out the way."

"Pub"? said Phartman, "I went to find some food for Nik Nik, and I got asked to go into a house full of people.

I think the owner was called Steve; he must be popular."

"That's the landlord," said Charlie.

Phartman looked surprised, "He's a lord? Wow I didn't realise, no wonder he was popular. I've read about your lords; I must go back and say hello."

"They said you drank quite a lot of beer last night," said Charlie

"Beer is that what you call it, they kept giving it to me, they gave me some small arrows which they said I had to throw at a small, coloured round board on the wall. Several other people came and did the same. Then they gave me more of the beer as you call it. I think the game is called jammy or lucky devil," said Phartman.

"It's called darts," said Charlie, "Apparently you ate the flower display as well."

"Everyone was eating food from the table in the room, so I helped myself to the flowers, was I not supposed to?" said Phartman, sounding surprised.

"No", laughed Charlie, "They were for display, but don't worry Steve's wife thought it was hilarious. They want you to go again, but that wouldn't be a good idea. Rowland Butter from the local paper has been asking questions about you but I've managed to convince him it was a hoax."

"Well, I did play a few tunes in the bar, although they did ask me to stand next to the open window after the first tune. It was good, I played them the most popular song on Gaseous at the moment. It's called wilyfurttrumpenpoop, wonderful song", beamed Phartman.

"I'll take your word for it, I won't ask you to play it now", said Charlie.

"Well perhaps later then," suggested Phartman.

***

Geoff drove down to his cabbage field to see a young chap standing in the middle of the field.

"Hello I'm Roland Butter, from the Scroton Gazette. I've heard rumours that a

spaceman landed in this field."
Geoff, taken by surprise, tried to dismiss the claim.

"No, no, I've not seen any spaceman here, oh no. No, you must be mistaken," he spluttered.

"Well, where have all your cabbages gone then? You can't have sold them because of the cabbage blight going around," said Roland.

"Well, no, ahh, yes, no, err, ooh, ahh, well, oh yes they have gone for cattle feed," said Geoff, very unconvincingly.

"I didn't know cattle eat cabbages," said the young reporter.

"AAH, yes, well, these are special cabbage eating vegetarian cows," blurted Geoff.

"Veggie cows," exclaimed the young reporter.

"Oh, yes these are Argentinian long hair short horn mountain cows, they only eat cabbages." said Geoff, starting to feel more comfortable about his deception, as well as surprised at his own ability to come up with such an outlandish story.

Rowland looked at Geoff with a mixture of disbelief and curiosity, as he began to think that this would make a good article for his column in the Scrotun Gazette, and hopefully gain some brownie points from his editor.

"Great," he said, "When can I come and see them? It sounds like a good story for the paper."

Geoff's newfound confidence suddenly evaporated as he went into panic mode.

"Oooh, no. Well, no, aah, well they're scattered all over the valley, I haven't seen them for a while," stumbled Geoff.

"Well how do you know if they're OK?" asked Rowland in concern.

"Aah, well we have a homing device on them so we can track them," said Geoff.

"Good, can I see it?" asked Rowland.

"Err, I've lost it," said Geoff, who was very nervous now and blurting out the first things he could come up with.

"So how do you know where they are then?" asked Rowland, confused.

Geoff stood and looked at him for a few seconds, desperately wishing that an earthquake would suddenly erupt, and the young idiot would disappear down a deep hole. Geoff looked at his watch.

"Oh, is that the time? I have got to meet the vet back at the farm, one of the turkeys has got a limp. Sorry must go, nice to meet you, Ronald."

Geoff ran to his truck and made a quick escape back up to the farm. He kept an eye on the rear-view mirror to make sure has wasn't being followed.

Rowland Butter drove down the valley towards Scratchit Village, still pondering the conversation with Geoff. He was trying to think how he could make a story about Geoff's cattle, but he was a little hesitant, because his last story about an escaped zebra being spotted in Scratchit Meadow Farm, turned out to be a black pony that had been leaning on a freshly painted white fence.

The hapless reporter drove into the village and headed for the local pub, the Flying Pig. Trying to look inconspicuous, he walked into the bar and ordered a half pint of bitter. Frank, the landlord, recognised him straight away.

"Morning Rowland spotted any zebras lately?" he quipped.

Realising his cover was blown, Rowland decided to launch into reporter mode. "I've heard reports that you had a spaceman in here last night", stated Rowland.

"What!" exclaimed Frank. "Have you been drinking our Old Uncle Silas Head Banging Bitter?" Frank shouted across the bar to George, who was one of the regulars sitting in the corner.

"Did you see a spaceman in here last night?" Frank asked him.

George looked at Rowland.

"No but have a word with mad Eric. He said he saw some pink elephants outside the Post Office last week, he's probably in the field with your zebra," laughed the old man.

Rowland could see he was not getting a serious answer to his question from George.

"Well, what about the surprise trumpet player in here last night then?" he asked Frank, "You weren't advertising it beforehand."

"Trumpet player..." Frank pondered, "We had Alan on his mouth organ and Steve was playing the spoons, but there was no trumpet player."

"But Billy the park warden rang me to say there was a spaceman playing the trumpet in here last night," said Rowland, getting more desperate for the story to be true.

Frank laughed. "Well, apart from Billy being drunk last night, he's also madder than Eric. He's as mad as a box of frogs", said Frank.

"OK", said Rowland wearily, "I can see I'm not going to get a sensible answer from you two."

Rowland walked back to his car and sat thinking of the fame he would achieve if he could get a picture.

He drove back towards the Scroton Gazette office considering the reaction from his editor if he presented a story written from the information he had gathered. Would it be fame and glory or redundancy? The thought of getting sacked made him reconsider.

He decided to talk to Billy, the park grounds keeper, again to try get more details to verify the story. Rowland drove to the park, stopping near to the groundsmen hut. He found Billy standing in the distance, looking at the rhododendron bush on the right side of the playing fields. As he drew closer, he could see all the flowers at the bottom of the bush were missing up to three feet high. Billy turned to look at Rowland.

"See that?" he exclaimed, pointing to the rhododendron "I was walking through here last night and I saw something eating all the flowers from the bottom branches."

"WHAT?" asked Rowland, "What was it?"

"Dunno," said Billy, "It was dark. But it was about three feet tall, hairy, with bright yellow eyes. Frightened the life out of me."

"Well, what did you do?" asked Rowland.

"I threw a stick at it, but it just threw it back at me. Just missed me, angry little critter."

"Then what happened?" asked Rowland.

"What do you think? I ran off; I'm not coming in here again at night."

Rowland looked at the ground around the bottom of the rhododendron, he could see what looked like small children's footprints.

"Perhaps it was kids", he said.

"Well, they will get a good telling off if I see them again. But it was the eyes, that's what scared me, angry little devil. I don't want to bump into it again. I thought I saw it jump over the fence into the police station yard."

Rowland went back to his car. He sat inside contemplating what sort of story he could write. He came to the conclusion he would need a picture to convince his editor that the story was real.

***

Charlie walked into the back yard of the police station, Phartman's spaceship was not visible. He walked slowly towards where it should have been, reaching out with his hand in front of him, he stopped when he touched the invisible craft. Charlie felt a mixture of disappointment that it was still there, together with a slight sense of relief that it was, as he was getting to quite like his amiable extra-terrestrial friend. He wouldn't be so bothered if Nik Nik had gone though.

He knocked on the side of the spaceship roughly where the door should be, but no one answered. Charlie knocked again, and the door opened, but to Charlie's surprise Nik Nik stood there, still looking his angry little self, wearing his chef's hat, and holding some kind of tool in his left hand. Charlie took a step back.
    "Where's Pharty?" asked Charlie, hoping Nik Nik would understand.
 Nik Nik stood looking at him for several seconds before raising his left arm to point to the fence. Charlie looked at the fence then looked back at Nik Nik.

"You mean he has gone over the fence." Nik Nik started jumping up and down pointing to the fence.

Charlie put his hand up to his forehead.

"Oh no he's gone walkabout again."

Suddenly there was a whirring gurgling sound inside the spacecraft. Nik Nik looked down the corridor inside, then slammed the door shut. Charlie stood motionless for a few seconds before speaking into his radio.

"Alpha One to all units, Phartman is out in the village somewhere. Keep an eye out for him and bring him back to the station. That gormless reporter from the Gazette is trying to find him."

Charlie walked back into the police station intending to get the keys for the police pickup truck, when a call came over the radio.

"Bravo One, we have a report of an armed robbery at the Post Office, robber believed to be still on the premises." Immediately sirens could be heard outside, as police cars made an urgent dash towards the robbery.

Charlie grabbed his keys then raced after the other cars. He arrived to see the road had been blocked off by the other police cars. Graham (Bravo One) stood several feet away from the front door to the Post Office. He walked quickly to Charlie.

"Dave Sanders came running up to me and said a young chap came in saying he had a gun in his pocket and demanded Julie give him all the money from the till."

"Well, did he have a gun?" asked Charlie.

"I don't know for sure. Dave said he had his hand in his pocket pointing something that looked like it could be a gun. He got out of there pretty quickly."

"OK", said Charlie, "we have to assume for now he has a gun. Cordon off the street and I will call for the firearms unit to attend."

The street was closed off and people were told to keep well back. Charlie rang the Post Office.

"Hello Julie, it's Sergeant Randall, are you OK?"

"Yes", came the hesitant reply, "He's got a gun in his pocket; he wants all the money out the till and a getaway car outside in fifteen minutes," Julie continued calmly.

"Well stay calm, we have people on their way."

Over the next twenty minutes, Charlie kept talking to Julie, the armed robber kept asking for the getaway car and a small crowd had gathered down the road behind the police barriers. Charlie stood across the road still waiting for the armed response team to arrive when he heard a familiar voice behind him.

"Good morning Inspector. What are all these people doing here? Is there a street party about to happen?" Charlie turned to see Phartman standing behind him.

"Where did you come from? I was looking for you earlier", exclaimed Charlie.

"I was just out for a walk when I saw your police cars come round the corner. What are you doing?" asked Phartman.

"We've had a report that a man is trying to rob the Post Office. He's got a gun in his pocket and demanding all the money from the till", said Charlie.

"Why are you all standing outside?" asked Phartman.

"We are waiting for the armed response team to arrive, we can't go in if he has a gun," said Charlie.

"Well Julie must be scared," said Phartman.

"Yes, I know but we can't go in," said Charlie.

"Well let me go in, I can deal with him", said Phartman.

"No, you can't go in there", said Charlie holding up his hand at Phartman, but before Charlie could utter another word, Phartman bounded across the road and opened the Post Office door.

"Greetings my good fellow", he said as he casually walked into the Post Office and shut the door.

There were a few seconds silence before a loud rasping farting sound could be heard coming from inside the Post Office. This was followed by a green mist appearing at the windows which slowly rose to the top of the Post Office windows.

Charlie stood motionless at the Police barrier wondering what on earth was going on inside, all eyes were fixed on the Post Office, when a familiar voice came from behind Charlie.

"It's him, isn't it? He's in there, isn't he?" Charlie turned to see Rowland Butter, eyes wide open, pointing at the Post Office.

"He's in there isn't he?" repeated the reporter.

"Who's in there?" asked Charlie, "We've got an armed robber in there, trying to rob the Post Office."

But before Charlie could offer any other explanation, the reporter ran excitedly across the road.

"Stop him!", shouted Charlie, but it was too late.

Rowland had reached the other side of the road and thrust open the Post Office door. But then he stopped dead in his tracks, as a green mist quickly enveloped him. He didn't make a sound; he just sank slowly to his knees.

Just as he was about to hit the floor, an arm appeared from the mist and grabbed him by the collar. Phartman stepped out from the green mist, then sat Rowland on the pavement, resting his back and head against the wall.

Charlie ran across the road.

"What's happening? Is Julie OK?"

"Yes, yes Inspector, they are both passed out inside. Julies sat on a chair, the other young fellow is passed out on the floor", said Phartman.

"What about the gun?" asked Charlie.

"It was a banana in his pocket", said Phartman.

"Well, where is it now?" asked Charlie.

"I ate it," replied Phartman, "It was delicious."

"Oh dear", said Charlie.

He went to walk towards the Post Office door, but Phartman put his arm out to block the doorway.

"You had better wait a few more minutes," said Phartman.

But Charlie had already started to push the door open, he caught a slight smell of the green gas, he coughed then his eyes started watering.

Taking two steps back, he said, "OOOH WHAT'S THAT SMELL?"

Phartman stepped forward and proudly announced, "Ahh, that's a mixture of Gangleclack fruit, Nazasnoot and Pinkelfurt berries, we use that mixture to keep the Slotengoots away while we are collecting Glackensnort leaves on the Planet Winkledangle. They're incredibly good for treating Rishonthrax."

"I won't ask again," said Charlie.

By this time, the mist had cleared and Phartman said it was OK to go inside. Graham went inside to arrest the robber, who was now getting back to his feet.

Charlie checked to see that Julie was alright as she got to her feet.

"What happened? The last thing I remember is that chap saying he had a gun in his pocket and to give him all the money."

"Let's just say our out-of-town visitor came in and disabled him," said Charlie.

"Oooh, you mean Phartman. What a lovely man. He came in earlier to buy some roses, he ate them all before he left the shop, he said they tasted much better than the ones from the park."

"Well, he saved you from the robber, but it's best if you don't mention it," said Charlie.

"Oh, yes, right, OK," said Julie.
By now several other police officers had arrived. The robber was searched, then put into a police van to be taken back to Tollpiddle Police Station.
Charlie turned to Phartman.

You had better go back to your spaceship before Roland Rat here wakes up and sees you." Phartman looked at the sleeping reporter. Charlie checked to see that Julie was alright as

You had better go back to your spaceship before Roland Rat here wakes up and sees you.

Phartman looked at the sleeping reporter.

"He will be fine in a short while, he's happily sleeping. OK I'll go to see how Nik Nik is getting on with the Gronklespink converter, he seemed to think it was nearly complete."

With than he bounded off over the road and disappeared. Charlie went over to Rowland, still sitting with his back to the wall on the pavement. Charlie gave him a gentle shake.

"You OK son? You nearly collapsed." Rowland looked up to see Charlie standing over him.

"What happened? I remember opening the door, then it all went black," said Rowland, groggily.

"Ahh it was the robber. He knocked over a couple of bottles of cleaning fluid which smashed on the floor. The two liquids mixed together and gave off some nasty fumes, which caused everyone to pass out, but it's cleared now.

Everyone is OK. Except for the robber, he's been arrested and taken away. He was pretending a banana in his pocket was a gun – now there's a story for you".
    Rowland looked at him still a little confused. "What? A banana, are you serious?"
    "Definitely, he's round at the station now, if you want the details," said Charlie.
Rowland got to his feet, feeling a little better as his head cleared.
    "What about the spaceman?"
    Charlie looked straight at the irritating reporter. "Look there is no spaceman. You can't believe what mad Billy tells you, he's madder than a box of frogs. Why don't you go round the café and get a cup of coffee? Pop in the station tomorrow, then we can give you the details for your story."

Rowland looked around, all the police had gone, people were walking off in different directions. He put his pen and notebook back in his pocket, then considered what the story could have been.

But Charlie had told him it had been a hoax by a stupid robber, so he would have to be happy with that for his story. He walked back towards his car, leaving Charlie standing outside the Post Office.

Phartman leapt over the back fence into the police station yard, then entered the spacecraft. Nik Nik had completed the adjustments to the Gronkelbonkslapenfurt drive, telling Phartman that it worked perfectly and asking why they hadn't used cabbages before.

"Well, we must try them again next time we pass through this galaxy", said Phartman. They both started to make preparations for leaving.

***

The following day, Rowland called at Tollpiddle Police Station to gather the information on the hapless Post Office robber. He had interviewed Julie about the incident. He had hoped that he would get a serious story to write about.

It turned out to be a joke by a young student who had been dared by his friends to pretend to be a robber. But it had all gone wrong when another customer had walked in, then panicked before running out and calling the police.

The stupid lad had been given a serious warning about his behaviour and told he could be taken to court for wasting police time. Rowland was a bit disappointed it wasn't a more sensational story, but it would make a change from Ann Page's cat being rescued from a tree by the fire brigade, of Alf Bennet winning the best marrow prize in the annual village fete. He walked out the front door of the police station, then started heading to his car intending to go back to the office. But then he spotted Charlie coming out of a side door, heading towards the back yard of the police station. He decided to follow him to ask more questions about the Post Office robber. Rowland turned the corner into the back yard to see Charlie holding out his hand in front of him, he seemed to be patting the air in front of him.

Charlie moved slowly forward trying to find the invisible spacecraft. His hand touched something in front of him, and he tapped quietly on the side. To his surprise a door opened and Phartman stood in the doorway. Charlie was suddenly aware of footsteps running up behind him. He turned to see Rowland running at top speed towards him with his hand held out in front of him shouting excitedly, "ITS HIM, ITS HIM!". Charlie stood motionless holding up a hand in an attempt to stop Rowland. "NOOO", shouted Charlie as the young journalist rushed past. Unfortunately, Rowland had gathered considerable momentum, and was unable to stop. He ran straight into the back fence of the police station, banging his head before falling to the ground.

Charlie stood for a few seconds, before realising his intergalactic friend had gone. With a mixture of sadness as well as relief, he walked over to Rowland who was now picking himself up again, whilst rubbing his head.

"It was him, wasn't it?" shouted Rowland.

"Who?" asked Charlie.

"The spaceman, the spaceman!" blurted Rowland.

"You've had too many fizzy drinks, you should stick to tea", said Charlie.

"He was there!" protested Rowland.

"Have you got a picture?" asked Charlie.

"Well, no, I left my camera in the car," admitted Rowland.

"Oh dear, what a shame, never mind," said Charlie smiling.

"But he was there!" protested Rowland.

Charlie looked around the yard.

"There're are only three things in this yard: you, me and Jack Miles' old bike we pulled out of the canal", he said, "Now if you can get yourself up, it's best if you go. I've got a lot of things to do today."

Rowland shuffled off towards his car, Charlie breathed a sigh of relief. He stood for a few seconds reflecting on the last few days' events.

A smile came over his face as he thought about Pharty. It disappeared when he thought of Nik Nik, he wouldn't mis that angry alien with a bad attitude. He took one last look around before picking up a cabbage from the floor. Daves, rabbit will like that, he thought to himself as he walked back into the police station.

***

When Charlie woke the next morning, he sat up in bed thinking about his friend Phartman, wondering if he would ever see him again and wondering where in the universe he could be now. All the village had come together to protect Pharty from Rowland Butter. Although he did have some sympathy for him not getting his big story, he was glad they were not overrun by the world's press. He sat for a few more minutes before getting showered and dressed, then went downstairs to the kitchen, to pour himself a cup of tea. He looked out the kitchen window to see his wife, Abby, pegging out the washing in the back garden. He sat down at the kitchen table as Abby came in from the garden, holding a small strange-looking tube with some holes through it.

"I found this in your shirt pocket before I washed it. What is it?" asked Abby.

"Pharty" gave it to me, he didn't really say what it was for," answered Charlie.

Abby inspected it more closely.

"It looks a bit like a whistle", she said, blowing into it.

It made no sound; Charlie looked a little puzzled before his attention turned to a sound in the distance. He listened carefully, fast approaching and getting louder could be heard "Woof woof bark yap, wuf bark woof woof bark yap woof yap wuf wuf."

Charlie's eyes widened, thrusting out his arm he shouted, "SHUT THE DOOOR!"

About the author

As a child of the 50's I was brought up on the television programmes of Mr Pastry, The Marx Bros, Laurel & Hardy, Charlie Chaplin & many more.
Which is where my love of slapstick and the absurd comes from.

I get the biggest thrill from making people smile. With my writing, I hope to entertain, not just children but anyone who is still a kid inside.

https://www.glyndaviesbooks.com

Acknowledgments

I want to say a special thanks to the people who have assisted me in producing this book

Robin Davies

For his time in creating the front & rear cover artwork

https://www.robindaviesillustration.com

Sarha Khan

For editing my ramblings into a printable book

Graham Mack

For narrating and producing a brilliant audible version

https://www.grahammack.com/

You dear reader

Thank you for buying this book, I hope it makes you smile.

Printed in Great Britain
by Amazon